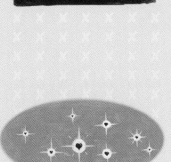

LOVE IS A FAMILY
ROMA DOWNEY

ILLUSTRATIONS BY JUSTINE GASQUET

ReganBooks *An Imprint of HarperCollinsPublishers*

For Reilly
with all my love . . .
Mommy

HarperCollins books may be purchased for educational, business, or sales promotional use. For information please write: Special Markets Department, HarperCollins Publishers Inc., 10 East 53rd Street, New York, NY 10022.

FIRST EDITION

Designed by Kelly S. Too

Printed on acid-free paper

Library of Congress Cataloging-in-Publication Data has been applied for.

ISBN 0-06-039374-2

01 02 03 04 05 ❖/WORZ 10 9 8 7 6 5 4 3 2 1

"I want a **real** family," said Lily,
slamming the screen door shut behind her.

"And what would that be?" her mama asked.

"More than just you and me! Tonight is Family Fun Night, and I bet I'll be the only kid in the whole class bringing just one person. What kind of a family is that?"

"A small kind," teased Mama. "But it's still a **real** family."

Lily didn't want to have a snack with Mama like she did most days after school. The house was **too quiet** and **too neat**.

"I'm going next door," she said.

Melissa's house was never quiet and never, ever neat. Melissa had four brothers and two sisters. She shared a room with her sisters, and every night they had a pillow fight before they went to sleep. When I go to sleep, thought Lily, all I get is the next chapter in the book Mama and I are reading together.

Lily played with Melissa in her noisy, messy house until Mama called her home to get ready for Family Fun Night.

Mama asked, "Do you want to call Uncle Mike and Aunt Lizzie to see if they'll meet us there?"

"Uncles and aunts don't count," Lily told her. "Sometimes I wish I had sisters or a dad who lived with me, or at least a brother or **something!**"

"I know," said Mama. "Sometimes I wish that, too. But most of the time our little family feels just right to me. **Love** is what makes a family, and we've got **plenty** of that."

Lily knew it was true. Even so, her lonely feeling wouldn't go away. She kept worrying about how they'd be the weirdest family at Family Fun Night.

But as it turned out . . .

When they got there they saw plenty of families that didn't look like Melissa's.

Lily talked to a girl who was there with just her dad. She came back and whispered to Mama, "Remi's mom died and she has **no brothers or sisters**, so it's just the two of them."

"That's how I grew up, too," said Mama. Lily had forgotten about that. It felt weird to think about her mom as a little girl.

"But **how could your dad** brush your hair and make it pretty?" she asked. "Did he know how to braid? Or get the barrettes even on both sides?"

"Grandpa learned to do those things because he was my daddy and he loved me," Mama said. "He also baked peanut butter cookies and planned fantastic birthday parties. He sang songs and told awful jokes when I needed cheering up. There are as many ways for families to show love as there are different kinds of families."

Lily pointed to a girl in her class. "Like Tamika. Her mom and dad showed love by adopting her . . . **and getting her a puppy** . . . and freezing that big wad of gum out of her hair with ice cubes instead of making her cut it."

Mama laughed. "And how about Josh and Tony across the street? They don't have parents now, but they have **grandparents** who pop popcorn for scary movies, rescue balls from the roof, pull splinters out of dirty fingers, and catch lightning bugs. I call that a family."

At **Family Fun Night**, they saw families with stepdads

and stepmoms and half sisters and half brothers. There were single moms

and single dads and families made up of different colors of skin. Everyone
was laughing and showing their love by being together.

But later—walking home in the cool night air—it was just Lily and Mama again, alone under a million sparkling stars.

Lily pointed. "See that big bunch of stars over there? That's how big Melissa's family is."

"That's a nice bunch of stars," said Mama.

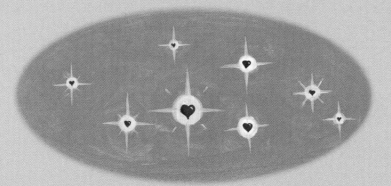

"Yeah, but look at those **two pretty stars** twinkling together over there," Lily said, smiling. "They're like us."

"They're shining just as brightly."

"Mama, someday you'll be old and I'll be grown up," said Lily. "And do you know who will brush your hair then? It will be me. And I'll braid your hair for you and I'll make sure the barrettes are even on both sides. Because **you and I will always be a family and we'll always have love.**"

Mama squeezed Lily's hand.

And those two stars shined like the **brightest diamonds.**